MISTER
MAGNOLIA

Quentin Blake

Jonathan Cape
London

Mister Magnolia was winner of The Children's Book Award
(Federation of Children's Books Groups) in 1981

Other books by Quentin Blake

PATRICK
ANGELO
QUENTIN BLAKE'S ABC
QUENTIN BLAKE'S NURSERY RHYME BOOK
MRS ARMITAGE ON WHEELS
ALL JOIN IN
COCKATOOS
SIMPKIN

Illustrated by Quentin Blake
with text by Roald Dahl

THE TWITS
THE BFG
ESIO TROT
MATILDA
THE ENORMOUS CROCODILE
GEORGE'S MARVELLOUS MEDICINE
DANNY, THE CHAMPION OF THE WORLD
THE VICAR OF NIBBLESWICKE
REVOLTING RHYMES
THE WITCHES
MY YEAR

with text by Russell Hoban

ACE DRAGON LTD
THE MARZIPAN PIG
HOW TOM BEAT CAPTAIN NAJORK AND HIS HIRED SPORTSMEN
A NEAR THING FOR CAPTAIN NAJORK
THE TWENTY ELEPHANT RESTAURANT

First published 1980

© Quentin Blake 1980

Quentin Blake has asserted his right under
the Copyright, Designs and Patents Act, 1988
to be identified as the author of this work

First published in the United Kingdom in 1980 by
Jonathan Cape Ltd
Random House, 20 Vauxhall Bridge Road, London SW1V 2SA

Reprinted 1981, 1983, 1984, 1987, 1991, 1995, 1999

A CIP catalogue record for this book
is available from the British Library

ISBN 0 224 01612 1

Printed in Singapore

Mr Magnolia has only one boot.

He has an old trumpet

that goes rooty-toot —

And two lovely sisters
who play on the flute —

But Mr Magnolia has only one boot.

In his pond live a frog

and a toad and a newt —

He has green parakeets

who pick holes in his suit —

And some very fat owls
who are learning to hoot —
But Mr Magnolia
has only one boot.

He gives rides to his friends

when he goes for a scoot —

And the splash is immense
when he comes down
the chute —

But Mr Magnolia
has only one boot.

Just look at the way that
he juggles with fruit!

The mice all march past
as he takes the salute!

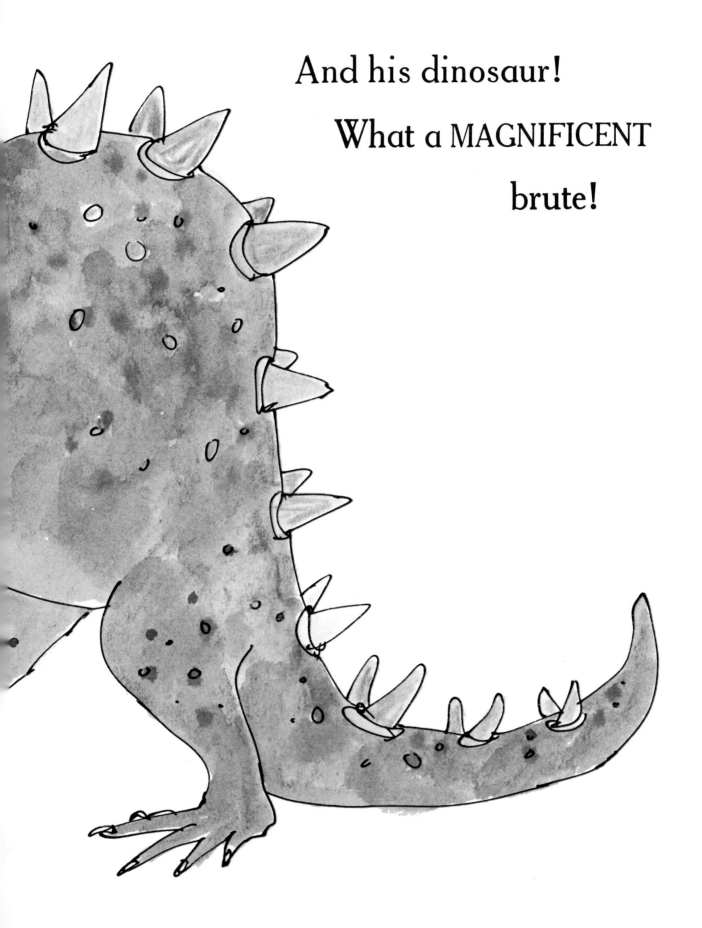

And his dinosaur!

What a MAGNIFICENT
brute!

But Mr Magnolia —
poor Mr Magnolia!
— Mr Magnolia
has
only one boot . . .

Hey —

Wait a minute . . .

Now then . . .

Keep going . . .

What's this?

Look!

It's a boot!

It's a boot!

Whoopee
for Mr Magnolia's
new boot!

Good night.